Napoleon Bonaparte
Napoleon Bonaparte, one of the greatest military leaders in history, was born in Ajaccio, Corsica in 1769. He was a talented writer of short stories and essays. He died in 1821.

Peter Hicks
Peter Hicks is a historian specialising in Napoleon. He is Manager of International Affairs at the Fondation Napoléon and a visiting professor at Bath University.

Émilie Barthet

Émilie Barthet is a graduate in French Literature and Information Science. She was editor-in-chief of Napoleon Bonaparte's correspondence at the Fondation Napoléon until 2007, and is curator of books at l'Université Paris Descartes.

Armand Cabasson

Armand Cabasson, a psychiatrist working in the north of France, is the author of several novels and short stories, including the Quentin Margont series of thrillers set in the Napoleonic Wars. The second in the series, *Chasse au loup* (published in the UK in May 2008 as *Wolf Hunt*) was awarded the 2005 Fiction Prize by the Fondation Napoléon. Armand Cabasson is a member of the Souvenir Napoléonien.

CLISSON
AND
EUGÉNIE

CLISSON
AND
EUGÉNIE

NAPOLEON BONAPARTE

TRANSLATED BY PETER HICKS

Gallic Books
London

A Gallic Book

First published in France as *Clisson et Eugénie* by Fayard
Copyright © Librairie Arthème Fayard, 2007

English translation copyright © Gallic Books 2009

First published in Great Britain in 2009 by Gallic Books, London

This edition 2024

A CIP record for this book is available from the British Library

ISBN 978-1-906040-27-7

Typeset in Fournier MT by SX Composing DTP, Rayleigh, Essex

Printed and bound by LSI

CONTENTS

INTRODUCTION

I was delighted to be asked to write this introduction to the Gallic Books edition of *Clisson and Eugénie* because I believe the text to be key to the understanding of Napoleon the man.

Clisson and Eugénie is a novel written by Napoleon Bonaparte. Of course everyone has heard of Napoleon I and his innumerable military triumphs, but fewer people are aware of his prowess as an author.

The novel has already been published several times in France, accompanied by explanatory documents, postscripts, notes and commentaries. The challenge for me, therefore, was to see if I could find something new to say about it. As well as being passionately interested in the Napoleonic period (and it is the period that has hitherto interested me more than the character of the man himself, which I regard somewhat critically), I am also a psychiatrist and an author, many of whose books are set in the Napoleonic era. Since most of the commentaries so far have been written by historians, I was keen to discover what my perspective as author and psychiatrist could add to the reading of the work.

There exists what I like to call 'the Trial of Napoleon'. Everyone is on the jury, since everyone has an opinion about the great man. Even two centuries after he died, it is true to say that few people are indifferent to Napoleon. The various opinions of him differ widely. Was he a plague on humanity or simply the whipping boy of a troubled era? The saviour of Revolutionary ideals who ultimately failed, or a classic military dictator of the type that history throws up from time to time? Some call him an atypical dictator, many a military genius. Was he a victorious general who, like Alexander the Great, showed himself incapable of renouncing military action? Or a lucky general adept at taking credit for the successes of his excellent officers? A tyrannical over-protective father? The perfect illustration of the corruption of power, which turned a sincere republican general into a tyrant? A pathological risk-taker (witness the 1812 Russian campaign, which was nothing more than a giant toss of the coin, demonstrating an incapacity to say: that's enough, I'll stop here)? A misunderstood visionary reformer? The 'republican' and 'imperial' variant of a king crowned as a result of a military coup? And the list of interpretations goes on . . .

Napoleon is still an enigma even after more than fifty thousand books written about the era, and by and about the man himself.

Of those fifty thousand books, *Clisson and Eugénie* is one of the most revealing.

Napoleon wrote some works (including several short stories) when he was still Bonaparte. But *Clisson and Eugénie*, written in the autumn of 1795, remains his most successful and important work of fiction. His other noted work of fiction is *The Memorial of St Helena*, dictated, or perhaps merely recounted in an informal manner, to Emmanuel, Comte de Las Cases, during the years of captivity on St Helena. It might seem odd to refer to *The Memorial of St Helena* as fiction rather than a memoir, but in fact it has long been recognised that rather than dictating his life story, Napoleon was constructing his legend, transforming his life into myth. *The Memorial of St Helena* is a sort of autobiography, but fictionalised and embellished for posterity. And it was more successful in creating the legend than Napoleon could ever have imagined. Still today, a number of ideas about what Napoleon was like are based more on the narrative of *The Memorial of St Helena* than on reality. This is not a new phenomenon. In England, Richard III will for ever be known as a bloody machiavellian dictator because that's the way Shakespeare depicted him. Even if historians and writers produce solid arguments to show that he was probably not the odious murderer of his brother Edward IV's two young children, we continue to believe he was their murderer in spite of everything. Shakespeare says so! (Readers interested in the question of Richard's innocence or otherwise will enjoy reading Josephine Tey's excellent novel *The Daughter of Time*.) It is said that 'the pen is mightier than the sword'; alas, this is not always true, but the pen is in any case mightier than reality . . .

So Napoleon's life is marked by two key pieces of creative writing, one written in 1795 before his rise to power, and the other written from 1815–1816 after his reign was over. They form significant signposts to his life.

The style of *Clisson and Eugénie* is very striking. The sentences are frequently short, concise and trenchant. It is exactly the same style that Napoleon continued to use once he became emperor, for giving orders, for dictating the famous Grande Armée bulletins that informed the world of the outstanding feats of his troops (and in which truth and propaganda featured in equal measure) or for crucifying someone with one of his famous insults. A celebrated example of such an affront came at the end of an interview with Talleyrand, whom he rightly suspected of being a traitor. Napoleon drew the meeting to a close with the words, 'You are nothing but shit in silk stockings.'

There are two things to point out about the story's abbreviated style. The first is that it is not easy to write in such a way. It is no easier to compose concise sentences than long ones and it takes as much skill to write sparely as to create prose that is liberally laced with metaphors. So a terse pared-down style requires as much talent as the ornate flowery style espoused by many contemporary French writers.

It is quite obvious that *Clisson and Eugénie* has been worked and reworked many times. Napoleon spent hours and hours on the story, take it from me, another writer. So the book is not just the hasty scrawl of a general, bored in his barracks; it is a work that haunted the man, that exhausted him, that tormented him until he had the correct sentences down on paper. One should not be misled by the unfinished appearance of the story. True, there appear to be little things missing, and certainly the work was not fully finished. But there is enough evidence from the versions left to posterity that Napoleon worked at and polished the writing several times, and that the opening at least was very close to the final version, had Napoleon been able to finish it.

The second point to note is the astonishing contrast

between the brief, rapid, precise style, and the passages that suddenly soar into lyricism. Some passages are firmly anchored in reality; they talk about concrete things in a narrative without embellishment. Sometimes, however, Napoleon's imagination carries him off into the lyrical. The result is a story that is bittersweet, combining two flavours that it seems to me were not normally linked at that time.

As Peter Hicks and Émilie Barthet have shown here in the interpretation, the novel is impregnated with Romanticism (using the term in the sense of the emotional and artistic movement that flourished in Europe in the eighteenth and nineteenth centuries, and which is still alive and well today and continuing to inspire and draw forth excellent works). Napoleon romantic? Who would have thought that those two words would go together? Not me, at any rate! And yet that's the conclusion one reaches on reading the novel. *Clisson and Eugénie* is in many ways similar to *The Sorrows of Young Werther*, one of Goethe's masterpieces, published in 1774. Napoleon admitted that he had read that novel seven times. We know that he read it six times during his Egyptian campaign, from 1798 to 1799. When else did he read it? Was it before he wrote *Clisson and Eugénie*? I have not been able to establish that for certain, we can only speculate. *The Sorrows of Young Werther* remains one of the novels that best addresses the central themes of Romanticism (still using the term in the eighteenth-/nineteenth-century sense): the great human emotions, including of course amorous passion, but also the suffering of the soul, and that strange psychological state that we call 'melancholy', a word that covers a multitude of meanings. It is interesting that the word 'melancholy' appears twice in the space of a few lines in *Clisson and Eugénie*. The manner of this repetition seems worthy of note, and I think one can conclude that the theme was very important to the author and that the repetition was deliberate.

Let's leave the question of style now and deal with the plot. Can an author invent a character who is not based on himself? To this day psychiatrists, psychologists, psycho-analysts and writers cannot agree on the answer to this question. Perhaps it is not possible to give a universal response; perhaps each case should be considered on its own merit. So is Napoleon Clisson? And if the answer is yes, to what extent? For if *Clisson and Eugénie* can be read as a piece of fiction (and indeed must be read as fiction), it is obvious that it is also an important guide to under-standing the man Napoleon was. Every reader will draw his or her own conclusions, but I would like to point out certain things and propose some hypotheses for debate.

It has to be said that the novel contains some disturbing

autobiographical elements. Clisson is a brilliant general endowed with a dark side: he's fascinated by war. This worrying facet of his character is on display in the very first sentence of the story: 'From birth Clisson was strongly attracted to war.' A very old French tradition dictates that the opening sentence of a story must be particularly striking, and in fact that tradition is still alive and well among French novelists today – it is always a pleasure to open a book and read just the first sentence to see whether the book will appeal or not. As an aside, I'm not sure that the majority of English and American writers are so consumed by the importance of the opening sentence, but certainly in France the first sentence of a novel is already a novel in itself. So is it the case that Napoleon Bonaparte, an avid reader of his contemporaries' novels, had noticed this as well? Whether or not he had, Napoleon's opening sentence is very important.

The novel begins with Clisson's fascination with war, but as the story develops, this recedes into the shadows and is forgotten, and does not return to the forefront of the narrative until the climax of the story. Clisson meets Eugénie and rapidly falls in love with her. Eugénie is the second autobiographical element. Napoleon Bonaparte was indeed very much in love with an Eugénie: Eugénie Désirée Clary, better known today simply as Désirée

Clary. Their brief liaison lasted from 1794 until the first half of 1795, before gradually dying over some months. *Clisson and Eugénie* was written in the autumn of 1795, coinciding exactly with the end of the love affair. There are several different versions of their break-up, but it is often stated that it was Eugénie who tired of Napoleon Bonaparte first, to his great chagrin (witness the letters he wrote to his beloved, complaining of the long gaps between her letters to him). In late 1795, however, Bonaparte fell in love with Joséphine de Beauharnais and that put a definitive end to any chance of a reconciliation between him and Eugénie Désirée Clary.

There is another element that points to the fact that Napoleon strongly identified with Clisson. Clisson's spirit is a battlefield where Eros and Thanatos, love of life and fascination with death, confront each other, and this conflict infuses the whole story. Of course this could just be because it is such a universal theme, a reflection of the struggle that exists in us all. Or the depiction of that struggle could reveal an important truth about Napoleon and his era.

I will return to that question in the Afterword to the text of *Clisson and Eugénie*, translated into English by Peter Hicks.

Armand Cabasson

CLISSON AND EUGÉNIE

NAPOLEON BONAPARTE

FROM birth Clisson was strongly attracted to war. Whilst others of his age were still listening avidly to fireside tales, he was ardently dreaming of battle. As soon as he was old enough to bear arms, he took part in military campaigns, always distinguishing himself with acts of gallantry. Although still a boy, his natural ability and his love of action led him to attain the highest rank in the Revolutionary National Guard. Soon he had even exceeded the high expectations people had of him: victory was his constant companion.

But envy and all the petty jealousies that growing reputations attract, which ruin so many able men and so often stifle genius, brought false accusations against him. His cool head and moderation in the face of these attempts to sully his name served only to increase the number of his enemies. They said that his magnanimity was pride, that his firmness was insolence; even his triumphs were held against him and used as pretexts to bring him down. He began to tire of serving men who did not value him. He felt the need to retreat into himself. For the first time, he turned his gaze upon his life, his inclinations and his situation. Like all men, he desired happiness, but he had found only glory.

This turning in on himself, this introspection, caused Clisson to realise that he was not just interested in war and that he had other inclinations than to cause destruction. It was as important to nurture and improve the lot of men, and to make them happy, as to destroy them. He desired a period of reflection to try to sort out the host of new ideas that for several days had been besieging his soul.

He left the army camp and went swiftly to seek the hospitality of a friend in Champvert, near Lyons. The man's estate, on one of the best sites near that grand town, combined all the beauty that art and fair nature could produce.

Clisson stayed with his friend, trying to determine how he might find happiness, now that he had abandoned his illusions of glory. He did not spend much time inside the house. His friend very often entertained, receiving guests of high rank and station, and Clisson found the petty formalities irksome. A man of his fervent imagination, with his blazing heart, his uncompromising intellect and his cool head, was bound to be irritated by the affected conversation of coquettes, the games of seduction, the logic of the tables and the hurling of witty insults. He could not see the point in scheming and did not appreciate wordplay. His life was solitary, and he was completely bound up by a single thought, which he had not yet been able to formulate or to understand, though it overpowered his whole being.

Since he was accustomed to hardship, he needed action and plenty of physical activity. No occupation brought him greater pleasure than to wander in the woods. There he felt at peace with himself, scorning human wickedness and despising folly and cruelty. Clisson was surprised to find himself enchanted by the sights he saw. The birth and the close of day, the course of the evening star as it cast its silvery light over copse and field, the changing seasons, the varying vistas, the concerts of birdsong, the murmuring waters – everything struck him as if he were seeing it for the first time. And yet he was looking at things he had seen a thousand times before without ever having been affected in this way. *How miserable he had been in his previous life. Not only had he witnessed the destruction of his fellow men but he had also been punished because his soul, victim of illusion, excitement and apprehension, had been blind to the beauties and insensible to the pleasures of nature.*

Since he was naturally sceptical, Clisson became melancholy. In his heart, reverie had replaced reflection. He no longer had anything to work towards, to fear, or to hope for. This state of tranquillity, so new to his spirit, might quickly have become stupor, without his being aware of it. From dawn to dusk, as he wandered in the countryside he was moved by the plight of the unfortunate people he came across, and lent them a helping hand.

The spa baths at Allès are about one league from Champvert. Many people went there to enjoy the coolness of the climate. Right from the start he saw this place as a landscape of emotions. It was a realm of enchantment, and he missed not a single day. Unknown as he was, he wandered amongst the throng of 'hearts'. He gazed with interest at the beauty of the women and their dresses, mostly made of linen. People feel comfortable while taking the waters and he was able to engage in a great number of conversations (inconsequential in themselves but a contact nevertheless), which brought him relief from his melancholy and solitude.

One day when it had rained the day before, there were very few people at the spa. He noticed two young women who seemed to be enjoying themselves as they took their stroll; they walked with the lightness and energy of sixteen-year-olds. Amélie had beautifully set eyes, a slender and elegant figure, a bright complexion, a slightly oval face and an alabaster-white neck; she was seventeen. Eugénie was a year younger and not as pretty. When Amélie looked at you she seemed to be saying: 'You find me pretty; perhaps you are even in love with me. But you should know that you are not the only one; and you will only attract my attention by flattering me. I like compliments, and I love allowing people to make them to me.'

Eugénie never looked at a man directly. When she gave her sweet smile, she revealed beautifully arranged pearly white teeth. If someone made as if to take her hand, she would proffer it timidly, but then take it away again as quickly as possible. It was as if she were afraid to show her pretty hand, where the blue of the veins contrasted with the whiteness of her skin. Amélie had the same effect as a piece of French music that everyone listens to with pleasure because they appreciate the succession of chords and are soothed by the harmony. Eugénie, on the other hand, was like a piece by Paesiello which transports and elevates only those souls born to appreciate it, leaving

Eugénie for not having hidden the displeasure that the stranger's conversation had inspired in her. Amélie found him sombre but distinguished-looking and refreshingly honest. Eugénie thought that Amélie had been too open with him. Her heart was troubled, and she believed that her unease stemmed from a great aversion she had conceived for the stranger; she could, however, find neither explanation nor justification for her aversion.

The next day, Amélie tried in vain to get Eugénie to agree to come to the spa, stubbornly pressing her case. But Eugénie would not countenance it and rose immediately on Amélie's departure to write to her sister and then to walk around the estate.

Clisson was there already when Amélie arrived; and they picked up again like old friends. The freedom of the spa and the relaxed holiday atmosphere banished all formality and etiquette. They stayed several hours together, looking critically at the women in love; and the amiable, beautiful and charming Amélie returned home having formed an excellent opinion of Clisson. It was true she did not find him particularly seductive, but he was pleasant. She spoke only of Clisson all day long and persuaded Eugénie to take the waters the following day. Eugénie, meanwhile, had meditated a great deal upon some of the things the stranger had said; she did not know whether to hate him or to be impressed by him.

The day before, Clisson and Amélie had tacitly agreed to meet. Clisson was careful not to miss the assignation. But when from afar he saw Amélie approaching, he was annoyed to see her with her friend. Eugénie, for her part, listened but either did not reply or answered indifferently. She fixed her eyes on the stranger's, and never tired of looking at him. 'What is the matter with him? How sombre and pensive he is! His glance has all the maturity of old age, but his physiognomy reveals the languor of adolescence.' And then Eugénie became angry to see him so absorbed by Amélie. She feigned tiredness and persuaded the group to turn back to their country house. Here they were met by her doctor, who visited them from time to time. The doctor was astounded to see Amélie with Clisson, whom he did not bother to greet, although Amélie introduced him with the words 'Monsieur Clisson'.

'Excuse me,' said Eugénie to Clisson, interrupting Amélie's introduction, 'we have heard so much about you, I would very much like to get to know you better.' The sound of her voice and her physical appearance spoke to Clisson's heart and he looked at her more attentively. Their eyes met. Their hearts fused, and not many days were to pass before they realised that their hearts were made to love each other. His love was the most passionate and chaste that had ever moved a man's heart. Eugénie, who had hitherto dedicated her heart to friendship, who had thought herself insensible to love, felt the full blaze of it. Clisson no longer pitied himself, no longer worried about other men, enemies and war. From now on he lived only for Eugénie.

They met frequently. They often felt as if their souls were one. They overcame all obstacles and were joined for ever. All that is the most honourable in love, the tenderest feelings, the most exquisite voluptuousness flooded the hearts of the two enraptured lovers. They abandoned themselves fully to the healthy temptation to confess their love, to pour out their feelings tenderly and to join together their hearts, their thoughts and their souls. Gentle tears, their souls' bonds, guaranteed their happiness.

Clisson forgot about war and despised his former life when he had lived without Eugénie, without drawing every breath for her. He gave himself up to love and renounced all thought of glory. Months and years sped by like hours. They had children and remained deeply in love. Eugénie loved as steadfastly as she was loved in return. There was no sorrow, no pleasure or worry that they did not share entirely. You would have said that nature had given them the same heart, the same soul, the same feelings. Every night Eugénie slept with her head on her lover's shoulder, or in his arms. They spent every day together, bringing up their children, tending their garden and running their household.

In his new life with Eugénie, Clisson had certainly avenged the injustice of men. Indeed, he barely thought of it any more; it seemed to him like a dream. The world, the people around them, their neighbours had completely forgotten what Clisson had once been. Eugénie and Clisson lived a secluded life, delighting in love, nature and rustic simplicity. Some thought them mad, others misanthropic, only the poor appreciated them and blessed them, which consoled them for the disdain of fools.

Though she was already twenty-two, Eugénie felt as if she were still in the first year of her marriage. Never before perhaps had the aspirations of two souls been so perfectly bonded; never had love, in all its caprices, united two such different characters.

Life with a man as talented as Clisson had been the making of Eugénie. Her mind had become cultivated and her exceedingly tender and weak emotions had taken on the strength and energy required of the mother of Clisson's children. Clisson himself was no longer gloomy or sad. His character had acquired the gentleness and graciousness of his beloved. Military honours, which had accustomed him to high command, had made him haughty and sometimes harsh; Eugénie's love now made him more sympathetic and more flexible. They saw few people, and they were not well known even to their neighbours; their only contact with the outside world was when they helped the poor.

It was at the beginning of their seventh year of marriage, in short when the family was still young, that the bonds of their love were strengthened by the joy of children.

The heat was excessive. A terrible storm covered the horizon. Rain and flashes of lightning darkened and illuminated the sky. Eugénie burst into tears, oppressed by a dreadful pain. She clasped her beloved tightly to her breast. Sophie began to cry at her mother's pain, hiding in her skirts and hugging her knees with her little hands.

'My beloved, my wife, happy mother of my children, why, Eugénie, are your beautiful eyes wet with tears? You lack something; your heart is closed and empty! You often cry alone. You cry too when you are with the children. It is as if your heart were shut away in the corners of your soul. Wisdom and common sense seem unable to reach you.'

'The world is covered with thick clouds, scored by

lightning, thunder, torrential rain . . . My soul, like nature, is agitated.'

Eugénie, surrounded by her family, was in the grip of panic and she felt quite ill. Her heart was weighed down by pain. Clisson had gone hunting, and he came back soaked to the skin; he had been away for six hours. He tried to get his wife to look him in the eye, and he pressed his children to his breast. They were all sad; Eugénie felt oppressed and suffocated by the pain. He noticed this and his heart went out to her. Taking her in his arms, he spoke to her firmly.

'You are sad. And there are things that you keep secret from me.'

'My beloved,' she said to him, 'I did not wish to burden you with my pain. My soul is prey to ghastly premonitions. I see an impenetrable cloud before me, and it is sapping my power. Ah, Clisson! There is only one dreadful fate that could justify my panic, namely, that you stop loving me. If ever that happens, take my life with your own hands.'

Clisson, whom esteem, love and nature had tied irrevocably to Eugénie, used every means he could to bring her back to reason and happiness. He took Sophie in his arms.

'Dearest Eugénie, I swear to you, on the life of our

daughter Sophie, that I will love you for ever. But as for you, do not torture me. Must you invent reasons to panic when my heart is so tranquil?'

They prolonged their conversation into the night and the darkness, going to bed very late.

But just as they had fallen asleep, Clisson was awakened by the noisy arrival of a carriage and horses. He got up and saw one of his old couriers bringing him a letter from the government. It was an order to leave for Paris within twenty-four hours. There he was to be given an important mission, which called for a man of his talents.

Poor Eugénie! You sleep on as they take away your lover!

'So that is the explanation of this terrible mystery,' she cried. 'My dreadful fate is coming to pass. Oh, Clisson, you are abandoning me, and you are once again to be faced with the folly of men and the chances of fortune. Adieu, my happiness, adieu, happy days, so few and yet so infinitely cruel; and now so priceless.'

She was pale and weakened, and her voice faded. Clisson himself was hardly any calmer, but he had to go.

He was soon leading an army. But he did not take a single step without remembering Eugénie and recalling all the ways she had demonstrated her love for him. His name was the signal for victory and his talents and fortune raised him up. He was a success at everything; he exceeded the hopes of the people and the army; indeed, he alone was the reason for the army's successes.

Clisson, still so young and so important to his family and his fatherland; was he to die before his time?

He had been separated from his love for several years. But never a day went by without his receiving from Eugénie the most tender of letters, giving him strength and feeding his love.

One evening, however, Eugénie wrote to him: 'I am worried and unhappy. I feel numb. Come to me without delay. Only the sight of you will cure me. Last night I dreamt you were on your deathbed. The life had gone out of your beautiful eyes, your mouth was lifeless, you had lost all your colour. I threw myself on your body: it was icy cold. I wanted to revive you with my breath, to bring you warmth and life. But you could no longer hear me. You no longer knew me.'

On another occasion, Clisson wrote to her: 'You are ill. They told me the state you are in, although your letters and my premonitions had already given me a good idea. Last night I saw you sleeping, tormented by something, I know not what. The night before, I dreamt I was in your bedroom. I was watching over you. You were breathing your last, suffering the pains of death. I took your hand and bathed it with my tears. You came to and turned your head towards me. You recognised me, shook me and gave a sharp cry. You pushed me away indignantly. Then you turned your back on me, so as not to look at me any more. And when I awoke, I was in terrible pain, almost dead.'

In a skirmish, Clisson was forced into an exposed position and then seriously wounded; his renown served only to increase his woes. He dispatched Berville, one of his officers, to inform his wife that he had been wounded and to keep her company until he had made a full recovery. Berville was at the dawn of his emotional life. His heart had not yet loved. He was like the traveller who, exhausted and lost at the end of a long day's journey, casts his eyes around to find somewhere to rest for the night: he was looking for a place to lodge his heart. He laid eyes on Eugénie, he blended his tears with hers, he shared her cares; and all day long they talked of Clisson and his misfortune. He thought that his young heart – still a novice in emotional matters – was moved by sympathetic friendship. But a passion, all the more frenzied because it was hidden, unbeknownst even to himself, had seized him. He idolised Eugénie. She was not in the least on her guard with respect to her husband's friend.

Her letters to Clisson became shorter and less frequent. He began to be assailed by terrible doubts. He had now completely recovered from his glorious wounds, but he was troubled and could not hide the disquiet in his soul. Berville should have returned but he remained in Champvert. Nothing happened; Eugénie did not come. Her letters were unrecognisable and lifeless. Her soul no longer spoke to him. Eugénie no longer wrote to him, Eugénie no longer loved him.

Berville wrote him perfunctory letters, and even then only when he was obliged to do so. Night and day Clisson dwelt on his unhappiness, and his first thought was to rush to Champvert to snatch Eugénie from shame and dishonour. But how could he leave the army and his duty? The fatherland needed him here!

'My beloved, things are happening that I cannot explain. I say this trembling in fear and agony. Eugénie, your love has changed. Your heart has been stolen from me. Worse . . . this feeling is too harsh. You have been tricked. You are still virtuous, despite my absence and the wickedness of men. I no longer dare hope . . . My thoughts are all confused; perhaps my honour is gone.'

It was two o'clock in the morning. Everything was prepared for death. The orders had been given and the battalion was getting ready.

'Come the morning, this place will be soaked in blood! But as for you, Eugénie, what will you say, what will you do, what will become of you? Rejoice in my death, curse my memory, and live happily.'

The alarm was sounded at the break of day. The bivouac fires were extinguished. The columns moved out. Beating drums announced the charge on the flanks, and death stalked amongst the ranks.

'Only the wretched fear losing their lives and long to keep them! As for myself, I alone desire to end my life; for it was Eugénie who gave it to me.'

They came to tell him that the right flank had been overrun; a counterattack was under way. The centre had engaged and was locked in battle. Slightly later they told him that the centre had been victorious but that fresh troops were coming up to fight on the left.

'Adieu, you whom I chose as the arbiter of my life, adieu, the companion of my finest days! By your side I tasted supreme happiness. I have drunk of life and its goodness to the full. What is left for me in future days but satiety and world weariness? At the age of twenty-six, I have experienced to the full the fleeting pleasures of fame, but with your love I felt the heady emotions of the life of the soul. The memory of this is tearing my heart to pieces. May you live happily, and think no more about unhappy Clisson! Kiss my sons for me. May they not possess their father's passionate soul; otherwise like him they will only fall victim to men, glory and love.' He folded the letter, ordered an aide-de-camp to take it to Eugénie immediately, and, dutifully placing himself at the head of a squadron, threw himself headlong into the fray – at the point where the victory would be decided – and expired, pierced by a thousand blows.

TRANSLATOR'S NOTE

This text is an attempt at a faithful translation of the French text of *Clisson et Eugénie* as published by Fayard in 2007. Since it would appear that this text which has come down to us (apart from the first two paragraphs) was never the final version, a few passages remain that are incoherent and incomplete. These passages have been freely interpreted and completed by the translator. The most significant of these is marked in italics. For notes regarding these textual issues, please refer to the Fayard publication.

AFTERWORD

Now that the ending of the story is known it is possible to consider further the implications of Clisson's confusion between love of life and fascination with death. Napoleon ends his novel with Clisson, disappointed in love and desperate, plunging into a crucial battle and saving his fellow soldiers by throwing himself into the breach. He snatches victory from the jaws of defeat, but at the cost of his own life. He dies a heroic death.

Heroic death is a classic Romantic theme, and very often the death is suicide. It is disturbing to note that several famous people of Napoleon's era went to their death in a similar way to Clisson.

I am sure that English readers will think of the brilliant Nelson, who met his death on the quarterdeck of HMS *Victory*, the mortal shot fired by an élite sniper on the French ship *Redoutable*, as the Franco-Spanish fleet, that second 'Invincible Armada' was in the process of being broken up in front of his eyes. Why did he decide to wear his grand uniform with all his medals when it was obvious that such a fabulous outfit would make him an easy target for the marksmen, who were perched high up and from whom it was impossible to protect himself properly? The French marksmen had him within range. A simple service uniform would have been more discreet and would have allowed him to melt into the crowd of his officers, greatly reducing the risk of being hit.

The French reader, on the other hand, will be reminded of the flamboyant hussar general, Lasalle, who declared, 'Any hussar who's not dead by the time he's thirty is a blackguard!' At the battle of Wagram he charged at the head of a cavalry troop and his horse set off at such speed that it was impossible for the rest of the troop to catch up with him. He was struck down by a Hungarian grenadier, who was staggered to see a French general galloping on his own towards the enemy. His cavalry regiments thereafter bore the nickname 'Infernal Column' like the Wild Hunt of legend. Lasalle's spectacular end put the finishing touches to his myth.

There are many other names that could be cited in this tradition. And so the action Clisson takes at the end of the story is the enactment of a fantasy that was prevalent at the time: sacrificial heroic death in defence of a dearly beloved cause. In certain cases, those deaths were also reminiscent of the kind of suicide in which the victim asks someone else to help him kill himself, and that was clearly the case for Clisson. In *Clisson and Eugénie* (and I emphasise that this is only my own theory) the suicide also has an element of murder, Eugénie's murder. Because, since the story says nothing about what becomes of Eugénie, the reader is left to try to figure out what her reaction would have been to the announcement of Clisson's death. The man she had once loved, the father of her children, is dead. She had lived for several years with him, she knew him as well as anyone could (although no one can truly know another person, in fact one can't truly know oneself). His death would have made her realise the intensity of his feelings for her – he loved her more than he loved life itself. She would certainly have sunk into a state of devastating guilt. She would undoubtedly have contemplated suicide herself; the idea would have haunted her. So it is that the suicide of Clisson might have borne the seeds of the murder of Eugénie. The author tells us, 'From birth Clisson was strongly attracted to war.' And war is about killing someone else, not yourself.

Even though the conscious part of Clisson wanted

Eugénie to live happily (once he had realised that there was no hope of a reconciliation between them), the way in which he conveys this to Eugénie is insincere: 'Rejoice in my death, curse my memory, and live happily.' How could he genuinely have believed that the woman he loved, whom he continued to depict as sensitive and sincere, would be able to act in such a cynical and harsh manner?

And the hidden side of Clisson, the part that yearned for war, would have impelled him to end the love affair in the same way that a war is ended. Thus Clisson, by dying, was winning two battles: the tangible, military one against the enemies of his cause and the invisible battle of betrayed love. The circumstances of his death are in effect a way of whispering to Eugénie posthumously, 'You see, I loved you completely. Does my rival love you this much? Haven't you committed a terrible error in choosing him?' and equally, 'You see what you've done: you've killed me.' And that might have been the fatal blow for Eugénie. It is for each reader to imagine what might have followed on from Clisson's death, since the story is left open-ended. It is in some ways surprising that the story is entitled *Clisson and Eugénie*, since in fact Eugénie is completely ignored at the end. Perhaps it is because of this narrative imbalance that Napoleon at first envisaged that the story would be called simply *Clisson*.

over the bridge. Napoleon Bonaparte must have imagined what was about to happen; it must have seemed absolutely obvious: he was going to be killed and his grenadiers, mad with rage, were going to throw themselves on the Austrians to avenge him. The Austrians, having fired, would see swarms of French grenadiers, those giants of hand-to-hand conflict, coming over the bridge towards them, and they would flee. But suddenly the heroically suicidal scenario envisaged by Bonaparte faltered. His aide-de-camp, Colonel Muiron, spotted an Austrian aiming with precision at the young general . . . and just in time he threw himself in front of Bonaparte to receive the bullet instead. He died before the eyes of Bonaparte, who immediately took in what had just happened. Napoleon Bonaparte survived the attack, but only just. He fell off the bridge and found himself in the marshes below. In addition the French fell back; the mad charge had been nothing but a setback. Ultimately Bonaparte did win the battle, but thanks to another manoeuvre: he tricked the Austrians. It was less heroic and more intellectual, less dramatic, but considerably more effective as a strategy.

No one will ever know if he was planning to die on Arcole Bridge or if he was hoping that fortune, the lucky star he seemed to travel under, destiny, or I don't know what else would protect him. He would later maintain that it was that battle that made him realise that an extraordinary destiny awaited him. In any case, it is undeniable that the battle affected him profoundly. It is extremely rare to escape certain death because someone steps in to take your place . . .

Was that the great turning point in Napoleon's life? Was he a genuinely republican general ready to sacrifice himself for the ideals of the Revolution (in other words a Clisson) until that day on Arcole Bridge? Was it that experience that tipped him into his progressive evolution into the character of Emperor Napoleon? That's just speculation, admittedly. But it is our privilege to speculate and to try with the utmost rigour to imagine the missing pieces of the puzzle.

In any case it is impossible not to be struck by the great similarities between that moment in Bonaparte's life and the story he had written barely a year earlier. Napoleon Bonaparte must have felt that his fiction had come to life that day.

As for the rest of his life, let's give the last word to Napoleon. He said on St Helena: 'What an extraordinary novel my life would make!' And perhaps the novel that Napoleon Bonaparte inscribed in letters of blood in reality was actually the sequel to *Clisson and Eugénie*, a sequel in which Clisson survived by some miracle.

Napoleon's first known prose dates from the long hours he spent in the garrison of Valence, between 1786 and 1787. There was his two-page text *On Suicide*, dated 3 May 1786, which is an expression of nostalgia for life on Corsica. The author regrets having been separated from his homeland for 'six to seven years'. It seems that his disgust for France and his despair of his compatriots – 'cowardly, base, grovelling' – were his own sentiments and not those of an invented character. Secondly there was the famous passage (barely more than a page) dated very precisely 'Thursday 22 July 1787, Paris, Hôtel de Cherbourg, Rue du Four-Saint-Honoré' about a meeting with a prostitute from Palais-Royal – *A Meeting at Palais-Royal*. This piece relates one of his own experiences; it is intimate and specific, and is written in the form of lively dialogue. The last piece of writing from this period (apart from a rough draft entitled, very imaginatively, by Frédéric Masson and Guido Biagi *On Corsica's History*) is a comparison between patriotism and love of glory. This four-page text, written more formally, purports to be a response to an invitation from a young lady asking him to discourse on the aforesaid comparison. Using this framework, Napoleon evokes the works of eighteenth-century philosophers such as Diderot. Some have said that the rhetorical style of this piece of writing was inspired by that of his father, Charles.

In spite of the efforts of the young writer, none of these works found a publisher at the time. The texts are in varying degrees of completeness. It is clear that *A Meeting* and the comparison piece were unfinished, and *On Suicide* and *A Meeting* read more like long passages from a private diary than works intended for publication.

During the period that followed (1788 to 1789) Napoleon was posted to the Régiment de la Fère, garrisoned in Auxonne. He no longer lived in lodgings, as in Valence, but in barracks. His fictional writings in this period take a decidedly political turn. On 23 October 1788, he wrote the first paragraph of what would have become a dissertation on royal authority and which – one year before the Revolution – closes with this prescient sentence: 'There are very few kings who would not deserve to be dethroned.'

The Earl of Essex, An English Story also dates from this period. The title is underlined in the manuscript. The plot is drawn from John Barrow's *A New and Impartial History of England, From the Invasion of Julius Caesar to the Signing of Preliminaries of Peace, 1762,* which Napoleon read in French translation. It is a short, bloody tale of fantasy, set in the England of Charles II and based on the political history of that era. The ascetic Earl of Essex (explicitly compared to Cato, the incarnation of austerity) is plotting against Charles II but is in the end murdered. On the morning of the murder, the Countess has a premonition of her husband's death. She hurries off to the Tower of London where she finds her husband dead, his throat cut on the order of the Duke of York, the King's brother. The Countess is overcome with grief, only finding her revenge in the dethroning of the Duke three years later.

The Mask of the Prophet (the title, written in Napoleon's hand, has been underlined with great panache) is also a short story with a historico-political theme. This time, Bonaparte used as a model a short passage taken from *The History of the Arabs under the Caliphate* by Abbé Marigny, which he turned into a two-page story. It is the strange account of the charismatic prophet Hakem who, thanks to his beauty and his talents as an orator, is surrounded not only by loyal followers but also by his own army. Mahadi, the regional prince, is worried about the power of Hakem and his group. Hakem becomes disfigured by illness and, fearing that this change will disgust his followers, decides to wear a silver mask. The disguise is a great success and his disciples stay loyal. Hakem becomes more and more troublesome to Mahadi, who sentences him and his followers to death. The prophet has ditches dug and filled with lime, supposedly to trap his enemies. But he in fact intends them for his disciples, whom he poisons. He then throws their bodies into the lime, which consumes them, and lights a fire and immolates himself.

The last piece of fiction from this period is the famous *Corsican Story* (a title apparently invented by Masson and Biagi, the late nineteenth-century publishers of Napoleon's early writing). The story unfolds on a desert island and mixes elements of Daniel Defoe's *Robinson Crusoe* with the novels of Bernardin de Saint-Pierre. In spite of the very literary description of the island, the story concludes with a political tract on Corsican independence. Here, Napoleon seems to have been inspired by the works of Pasquale Paoli, Abbé Raynal and Rousseau, but, once again, he left the text unfinished.

What we learn from a reading of these literary essays is that Napoleon's style improved steadily from his first writings and that he was gradually increasing the complexity of his plots, inspired by what he was reading as he went along. His philosophical reading must have contributed to the clear style he ultimately attained.

It was only during the period from February to August 1791 that Napoleon began to give thought to writing his major work, *Discourse on the question proposed by the*

Academy of Lyons: what are the most important truths and feelings for men to learn in order to be happy? This was the subject of the composition prize organised by the Academy of Lyons and by Abbé Raynal, the famous author and literary correspondent of Napoleon's youth. The prize of 1,200 francs was undoubtedly attractive. Napoleon also asked for – and received – supplementary leave of six months in order to compete. The resulting composition is Napoleon's longest work, other than his official writings. The jury was unimpressed by his essay. One of its members, Monsieur Vasselier, described Napoleon's essay as 'a very pronounced dream', while the spokesman for the jury, Monsieur de Campigneulles declared acerbically, 'it is of little interest, too ill-ordered, too disparate, too rambling, and too badly written to hold the reader's attention'.

However, even in these first attempts at writing, it is possible to glimpse the author of *Clisson*. Napoleon also wrote, around 1791, a much more assured essay: *Dialogue on Love*. The *Dialogue* is a conversation, in the manner of *A Meeting at Palais-Royal* and, like the latter, is autobiographical. The conversation is between the author himself, referred to as B. in the manuscript, and Alexandre de Mazis, his friend from the École Militaire and the garrison. For the first time, love is the central theme. Mazis is depicted as impatient, full of himself and immature, whereas B. is the serene master of the situation and of the conversation. Although the dialogue is more an exercise in description of characters, the result is pleasing and much better than his previous works.

After *Dialogue on Love*, Napoleon started writing *The Supper in Beaucaire*, his most accomplished work so far. *The Supper* is a political pamphlet dated 29 July 1793, and defends the Montagnard stance in the conflict between the royalist Fédérés and the Montagnards in the Marseilles region. Once again, the work draws on Napoleon's personal experiences. He had been in the region during the Siege of Avignon alongside government troops, in General Carteaux's army, in order to take the town back from the hands of the Fédérés into which it had fallen. It is unlikely, however, that Napoleon met the four merchants in Beaucaire, near Avignon, where the text is set. In *The Supper* Napoleon describes a meeting in an inn at Beaucaire. A soldier from Carteaux's army, a defender of the Montagnards, who dominates the discussion, meets two merchants from Marseilles, only one of whom takes part in the discussion, and a man from Nîmes and a manufacturer from Montpellier. The soldier reasons with the civilians, emphasising the power of Carteaux's army and demonstrating the futility of resistance on the part of the people of Marseilles. He urges the civilians to yield to the Montagnards in the interests of the unity of the Republic. His argument is pragmatic: since the Montagnard troops will never be beaten, the people of Marseilles may as well negotiate with them. *The Supper* was sent to representatives of the Convention (the constitutional and legislative assembly), who agreed to finance its publication. The representatives approved of the oratory in the writing: the style was concise, elegant and effective.

Now the writer was mature enough to attempt his ultimate literary challenge: *Clisson and Eugénie*.

A Relationship is Formed

During the years 1794 and 1795, the period following Napoleon's ventures into literary and political writing, he was to experience the love affair that would inspire the creation of his most ambitious work, *Clisson and Eugénie*.

In the summer of 1794, Bonaparte, already a general of artillery, met Eugénie Désirée Clary, a pretty girl from Provence, and the sister-in-law of his brother Joseph, who had married Julie Clary on 1 August 1794. In the autumn of that year Désirée and Napoleon entered into an amorous, but platonic relationship, conducted mainly through letters. On 10 September 1794 Napoleon wrote: 'Dear Eugénie . . . the charms of your person and character have won over the heart of your lover.' On 4 February the following year he wrote to her about literature and her dancing. He urged her to learn music and offered to be her mentor. Then he wrote on 12 February 1795: 'If you could have seen, Mademoiselle, the emotions your letter inspired in me, you would realise the injustice of your reproaches.' Then again on 11 April 1795: 'I wrote to you, dear friend, from Avignon . . . Your image is engraved on my heart. I have never doubted your love, tender Eugénie, why would you imagine that I cannot love you any more?'

Napoleon then returned to Marseilles (on 21 April) apparently to ask for Désirée's hand in marriage. Yet this had not been discussed in the letters between the pair although Napoleon had written on 11 April of his commitment 'to you for life'. He left Marseilles on 2 May, arriving in Avignon on 9 May where he wrote to Désirée that he was 'much afflicted at the thought of having to be so far away from you for so long'. On 2 June he wrote from Paris, 'I saw many pretty women of agreeable disposition at Marmont's house in Châtillon, but I never felt even for an instant that any of them could measure up to my dear, good Eugénie.'

From 4 June 1795 onwards, however, relations between the pair were deteriorating: 'Adored friend, I have received no more letters from you. How could you go eleven days without writing to me?' wrote Napoleon. Then again on 7 June, 'I receive letters from all sides, from everyone but you, Mademoiselle.'

On 13 June 1795 Napoleon was appointed brigadier general of the infantry in the Western Army. But since he did not care for civil war, he managed to take a leave of absence from 15 June until 31 August for convalescence. That was how he had time on 14 June to write a long letter to Désirée, while she was in Genoa with her mother:

You are no longer in France, dear friend; were we not already far enough apart? You have decided to put the sea between us. I don't reproach you; I know that you were in a delicate position, and I was much affected by the touching picture you painted in your last letter of your troubles. Gentle Eugénie, you are young. Your feelings will first diminish, then falter, and some time later you will find yourself quite changed. Such is the effect of the passing of time. Such is the grievous, inevitable effect of absence. I know that you will always retain an affection for your friend, but it will be no more than affectionate esteem . . .

And Napoleon was right. On 24 June 1795 he wrote: 'It is a long time since I have had news of you, dear friend. Since you have been in Italy do you no longer think of those who are so passionately interested in you? If that is the case, you have changed very quickly.' Yet the young girl asked her sister and Joseph to send her a portrait of Bonaparte.

For his part Napoleon was now living a life in Paris that was leading him imperceptibly away from his 'dear Eugénie'. He wrote to his brother on 18 July 1795: 'Don't forget Mademoiselle Eugénie in spite of her silence and her absence in foreign parts.' On 30 July he again wrote to Joseph: 'My compliments to your brother-in-law, your wife, and also Eugénie, who no longer thinks about the inhabitants of Paris.'

In August, he changed his tone, urging Eugénie to forget him, while pretending that the thought made him forlorn:

No, dear friend, follow your instincts, allow yourself to love what is near to you. If you meet someone to whom your heart warms, at the sight of whom your soul is moved, and your reason yields, don't hold back, love and be happy. You know that my destiny lies in the hazard of combat, in glory or in death.

On 18 August 1795, Napoleon was sent to the topographical bureau at the Ministry of War. Towards the end of the month, he was assailed by other preoccupations than Eugénie and he thought of abandoning her. He wrote to Joseph on 25 August, 'I'll write to Mademoiselle Eugénie tomorrow.' Six days later, replying to Eugénie, his tone is noticeably less amorous and more straightforwardly friendly, as though their relationship were now just a pleasant memory: 'I received your charming letter, dear friend. It brought me great pleasure, as the memory of you always does. Often in the midst of the noisy pleasures this immense city brings, I think fondly of my dear Eugénie.'

From 31 August to 15 September 1795 he was attached to the Committee of Public Safety, in the section planning military operations and campaigns. His ambitions made him resolutely turn a new page in his life. On 5 September he wrote to Joseph, 'What must I do to end the Eugénie affair? . . . If I stay here . . . it's not impossible that I will be overtaken by the foolish idea of marrying . . . Perhaps it would be good to have a word with Eugénie's brother. If he is not in favour of it, let me know and no more will be said on the matter.' That was how, in Napoleon's mind, 'the Eugénie affair' was closed.

He was struck off the list of general employees by the Committee of Public Safety and on 4 October was appointed general of an infantry brigade and second in command of the Army of the Interior. This lasted until the 16th. It was in this capacity that he participated in the crushing of the royalist insurrection against the Convention, on the orders of Barras, the famous 'whiff of grapeshot' episode. On 11 October 1795 Fréron, an ally of the young general, mentioned Bonaparte in the Convention. Four days later he met Joséphine de Beauharnais. Towards the end of the year, he was promoted to general in command of the Army of Italy, before marrying Joséphine on 9 March 1796. He departed for the Peninsula on 11 March 1796.

Clisson and Eugénie is Drafted

The sequence of events outlined above led Simon Askenazy, the Polish historian, researcher and the first editor of the novel, to suggest that *Clisson and Eugénie* was written between September and November 1795. That hypothesis appears to be backed up by Napoleon's correspondence. Napoleon was impatient to bring 'the Eugénie affair' to an end, and the two 'fiancés' were separated geographically because that was what the young woman's mother and brother wanted, resulting in the definitive break-up. The split became a pretext for Napoleon to explore the theme of conjugal life in his writing. The plot he constructed went as follows: young Clisson, precocious, brilliant soldier, gives himself over entirely to war and the defence of his country. But the malicious rumours and gossip that come with his success make him flee public life. He retires to the country, sinks into melancholy and devotes his time to the contemplation of nature. But while he is taking a stroll near the baths of Allès, near Champvert, he meets two girls, Amélie and Eugénie, and is attracted to the former, more beautiful and livelier than her friend. The timid Eugénie is at first suspicious of him. But Clisson and Eugénie quickly become enamoured of each other and set out on family life, living happily and in tune with nature. After seven love-filled years Eugénie dreams that the family meet a dreadful fate. In fact the fatherland is in danger and has again called Clisson to combat. When he is injured he sends his aide-de-camp Berville to inform Eugénie and keep her company until he has recovered. The young passionate Berville falls in love with Eugénie and his love is reciprocated. Eugénie gradually stops writing to Clisson. Clisson, overwhelmed with grief, writes a farewell letter to his love and throws himself into the fray, where he is killed.

The Protagonists in *Clisson and Eugénie*

Napoleon drew inspiration for the names of his protagonists (Clisson, Berville, Amélie and Eugénie) from
his friends and entourage, but he enriched their characters
from his reading and nourished them with his aspirations.
Clisson's love of war and his brilliant military career were
certainly modelled on Napoleon himself. Like Clisson,
Napoleon studied the art of war early on (1779–1784); he
distinguished himself in his career while still young
(although not as young as Clisson) by fighting the British
successfully at Toulon. Like Clisson, this triumph was
then followed by disappointment, bitterness and 'the petty
jealousies that growing reputations attract'. In September
1795 (in the period when it is generally accepted that
Clisson and Eugénie was written) Napoleon's career was
stagnating. As he was not obtaining the rapid progress he
so desired, he used the imaginary Clisson to explore life
outside the army, a decision he did not dare to take
himself.

Why is the hero called Clisson? It was the family name
of one of his friends, Sucy de Clisson, that provided the
inspiration for his hero's name. His friend came from an
illustrious family, one of whose ancestors was Clisson
de Josselin, best known under the title of Constable de
Clisson. Constable de Clisson was close to Bertrand Du

Guesclin, French military commander during the Hundred Years War, and then succeeded him as Constable of France from 1380 to 1392. The role of constable was a peculiar one. He played the part of military adviser to the King, and was often in charge of an army corps; some constables of France also played a political role and led political factions. Constable de Clisson was famous for his bravery, his pride, his eternal sworn alliance with Du Guesclin, his love of the King of France and his fierce opposition to the English. After he was appointed Constable, Clisson was put in charge of the fleet for an expedition to England. There can be little doubt that Napoleon's hero was inspired by Constable de Clisson.

In 1798 Napoleon was in charge of l'Armée de l'Angleterre (bound for Egypt). He asked his secretary, Bourrienne, for about fifty volumes for his mobile library, including the two volumes of the *Life of Bertrand Du Guesclin*. Later in the camp at Boulogne on 16 August 1804, Napoleon invented a ceremony (coinciding with his birthday), by the sea, in full view of his English enemies, during which he himself awarded the crosses of the Légion d'honneur that were formally carried in on the armour of Du Guesclin and the chivalrous medieval knight Chevalier de Bayard. For Napoleon the name

'Clisson' therefore had strong patriotic and military connotations, and Constable de Clisson was undoubtedly a role model for the young Napoleon. The character in his story is thus a little bit himself and a little bit the person he wished to become.

The name 'Berville', Clisson's rival in the story, also comes from Napoleon's reading and his interest in Du Guesclin. *The Life of Bertrand Du Guesclin* appeared in two volumes in 1767, written by the historian Guyard de Berville (1697–1770). Berville's book is explicitly dedicated to students of military schools. It is simply written, and the historical facts are brought to life with the intention of providing young men with a role model capable of inspiring them to work hard, and to behave like gentlemen and warriors. The students were supposed to find in the book 'examples of bravery, goodness, and all the Christian customs and virtues, both civil and military'. We have already mentioned that Napoleon valued the work. He probably came across it at the military school of Brienne, where it was recommended reading. There is still a copy today in the Bibliothèque Nationale de France, which has a bookplate in Latin (dated 1787 – Napoleon left Brienne in 1784) stating that it was given to a student at Brienne as a prize for excellence in Latin translation, by Louis Berton, who also taught Napoleon. So it does not seem unrealistic to us to conclude that Clisson's rival was named after the historian Berville.

And finally there are the two young women, who were clearly identified by Simon Askenazy and the Napoleonic historian Gabriel Girod de l'Ain as being modelled on Julie and Désirée Clary. Napoleon's sister-in-law, Julie, with her firm character, inspired Amélie. Désirée reported that 'Napoleon once said to his brother Joseph, "In a good marriage, there should be one partner who always yields to the other. You, Joseph, are rather indecisive and so is Désirée, whilst Julie and I know our own minds. So you would be better off marrying Julie." Then, drawing me onto his knee, he continued, "As for Désirée, she will become my wife." And that's how I became Napoleon's fiancée.' Napoleon took Désirée's second name, Eugénie, for the name of his heroine.

A NOVEL

Although Napoleon's love life inspired him to write *Clisson*, the story's plot cannot simply be explained in autobiographical terms. The richness of the style, as exemplified by the forms attempted, reflects both the prevailing literary culture and the imagination of the author, who was, after all, a man of the eighteenth century, cultivated and curious. Although the fragmentary aspect of the story precludes any profound critical analysis, it is fair to see *Clisson* not just as a mere autobiographical sketch, but as a more complex composition, involving an interior portrait inspired by epistolary novels and Rousseauian reverie grafted onto the model of the pastoral novel.

Elements of the Epistolary Novel

Letters have pride of place in *Clisson and Eugénie*, and are used as a device to express feelings of love. Napoleon was adept at mixing up the genres as he ably demonstrated in

The Corsican Story in which he cleverly combined passages borrowed from Daniel Defoe, Bernardin de Saint-Pierre and Pasquale Paoli. In *Clisson and Eugénie* Napoleon punctuates his love story with dialogue conducted through letters or with references to letters the lovers have exchanged, in a manner that emulates the epistolary novel. Napoleon had read Rousseau's *Julie or the New Héloïse* (subtitled *Letters from two lovers living in a small town at the foot of the Alps*) of 1782 and found there a useful model for the expression of feelings. As Germaine de Staël would later say of *Delphine*, 'a novel in epistolary form always relies more on sentiment than events'. Perhaps Napoleon was also drawing on English epistolary novels, like *Pamela* by Samuel Richardson (1740). Not only was the plot itself constructed around letters ('But never a day went by without his receiving from Eugénie the most tender of letters, giving him strength and feeding his love'), but entire passages of the story are in fact letters. The Russian manuscripts, mentioned on pages 72–4, previously unpublished until the French edition, are made up of letters between Clisson and Eugénie. Clisson, in the army and wounded, writes to Eugénie, waiting for him at home, who replies to him full of anguish for their future.

Napoleon therefore carefully chose from various

genres according to what best suited what he was trying to say. When he wants to write about 'feelings', love and conjugal life, Napoleon follows the literary habits of the epoque and uses the epistolary mode. When he is writing about his preoccupations and reflections on the world around him, he prefers the narrative of reverie.

The Narrative of Reverie

Napoleon's text in parts describes his innermost feelings, using the narrative of reverie or dreaming. It is not strictly autobiographical, since it doesn't relate successive facts, nor does it deal with real facts. The author himself said, 'I often amused myself by dreaming and then measuring my dreams against reality. I would form an ideal world in my mind's eye and then try to work out how this differed from the world I found myself in.' That is why a large part of the text is devoted to the evocation of 'self' as expressed through reverie and the contemplation of nature: 'He felt the need to retreat into himself . . . he turned his gaze upon his life, his inclinations and his situation.' Rousseau's *Reveries of the Solitary Walker* (1782) was undoubtedly the model for the young officer. On the second walk Rousseau defines and explains the literary form he has chosen:

So having conceived the project of describing the habitual state of my soul . . . I could see no simpler or more sure manner of undertaking this enterprise than by keeping a faithful record of my solitary promenades and recording the thoughts [*rêveries*] that occupied me . . . These hours of solitude and meditation are the only time in the day when I am fully myself . . . and when I can really say that I am as nature intended.

Napoleon has Clisson remark that: 'Reverie had replaced reflection.'

The pastoral setting was essential for reverie or dreaming. It is in communing with nature that the true 'self' is revealed, like a rebirth:

Clisson was surprised to find himself enchanted by the sights he saw. The birth and the close of day, the course of the evening star as it cast its silvery light over copse and field, the changing seasons, the varying vistas, the concerts of birdsong, the murmuring waters – everything struck him as if he were seeing it for the first time.

The parallel with Rousseau is striking: 'Night was falling. I saw the sky, some stars and some greenery. The first sensation was a delicious moment,' he wrote in *Reveries of the Solitary Walker*.

The final theme of suicide in *Clisson and Eugénie* accords with this melancholy reflection on the self. In writing of suicide Napoleon was sharing the pre-occupations of his contemporaries – Goethe, for example, in *The Sorrows of Young Werther,* as mentioned by Armand Cabasson in his introduction. Suicide was very popular as a literary theme at the end of the eighteenth century and reached its apogee in 1835 with Alfred de Vigny's play *Chatterton*. Napoleon had written in a text in 1786, 'I am always alone even in the midst of men and so I go home to daydream on my own and give myself over completely to my melancholy' and 'Since I must die, should I not just kill myself?' And also punctuated his lamentations with the cry: 'How far from nature men have become!' In this way, by depicting his innermost thoughts and his aspirations through the contemplation of nature, Napoleon used nature as a symbol of purity and simplicity as opposed to the turpitudes of the city and public life. And by idealising nature, which is ever present in *Clisson and Eugénie*, he was also introducing both the themes and the style of the pastoral novel that was in favour all through the seventeenth and eighteenth centuries.

A Pastoral Novel

The major influence underlying the writing of *Clisson and Eugénie* is that of the pastoral novel. In eighteenth-century France, the genre was hugely popular, as shown by the success of works like Jean-Pierre Claris de Florian's *Estelle, a Pastoral Novel,* which tells of the love of the shepherd Némorin for the beautiful Estelle, and *Paul and Virginie* by Henri Bernardin de Saint-Pierre. The genre is characterised by three features: a natural, pure setting; a peaceful rural atmosphere; and themes of happiness and unhappiness in love.

Napoleon has all of these features in his story. The backdrop to the pastoral novel is nature untainted by civilisation. Napoleon followed the masters Florian and Bernardin de Saint-Pierre in this respect. The setting for *Clisson and Eugénie* is created around the aesthetic of '*la belle nature*', which is meant to be a moral allegory of happy humanity living in simplicity. Bernardin de Saint-Pierre renewed the taste for this at the end of the eighteenth century when in 1788 he published *Paul and Virginie*, the story of two island children whose love for each other, begun in their infancy, thrives in an unspoilt natural setting but ends tragically when civilisation interferes. The love story was so successful that it was published again (separately) in 1789. Napoleon was one of its most fervent readers. In the second volume of *The Memorial of St Helena*, Las Cases gives some significant clues to understanding Napoleon's taste in reading at the end of his life and corroborates his early enthusiasm for the work: 'In *Paul and Virginie* he loves the simple, touching, natural parts, rejecting those parts full of pathos, and the false abstract ideas which were so in vogue when the work was published, as being too cold and lacking in feeling . . . The Emperor said that he had been very taken with the book in his youth.' So it is hardly surprising that there are so many parallels between *Clisson and Eugénie* and *Paul and Virginie*, right down to the title. The descriptions of nature are similar, and in both works nature is depicted as the setting for a life that is authentic. While Napoleon described the setting for his story thus: 'The man's estate, on one of the best sites near that grand town, combined all the beauty that art and fair nature could produce,' Bernardin put it like this: 'All the workings of nature are aimed at the needs of man.'

As for the peaceful, virtuous atmosphere, Napoleon was again closely following his models. Florian, in his 1788 prelude to *Estelle*, explains how the pastoral novel mixes knights and shepherds and is written in a simple style, reflecting the naïve outlook of the characters whose 'only eloquence comes from the heart', but also in a noble narrative of reverie, and the pastoral novel. Although the novel is a mosaic of different literary models and is made up of disparate pages of manuscript, the resulting portrait is none the less coherent and moving. Through the descriptions of his innermost emotions, Napoleon delivers a story that is resolutely lyrical and is the last manifestation of an incipient Romanticism in a man who would go on to dazzle with his brilliant pragmatism.

de Malmaison, the final home of the Empress Joséphine. On 22 November 1821 Soulange-Bodin gave the fragment of manuscript to an unknown Anglophone, whom Hicks and Barthet have been unable to identify. A scrap of paper attached to the manuscript has the words: 'The writing of Napoleon Bonaparte given to me by his late steward at Malmaison on 22 Nov. 1821.' It next came to light when it was put on sale at Sotheby's in London on 26 July 1938 in lot 364. At that point the writer Stefan Zweig identified the manuscript as a passage from Napoleon's youthful novel and recommended its purchase to Heinrich Eisenmann, who bought it for £64. The document was then submitted to a curator at the manuscript department of the Bibliothèque Nationale for evaluation. The curator identified it as a passage from *Clisson and Eugénie*. Eisenmann then entrusted it to Paul Gottschalk to be sold in New York but it did not attract any buyers. Parke-Bernet Galleries put it up for sale for $2,500. It is not known who bought it, but in November 1957, it was found in the possession of the Cuban Julio Lobo. Unlike the rest of his Napoleonic collection, the fragment was not part of the Lobo museum at the time of the Cuban Revolution. Its next appearance was in 2005 in Milan, at the shop of the Italian autograph dealer Fausto Foroni. This part of the manuscript was unpublished until

Napoleon's generals, and Hugues Maret, Duc de Bassano, Napoleon's foreign minister from 1811 to 1813. This second part of the manuscript was first published in 1920, and several times thereafter, notably by Simon Askenazy in 1929 and in the periodical *Nouveau Fémina* (1955).

The third part (3) was a four-page manuscript, which appears on pages 18–23 of this edition, and which changed hands among well-known antiquarian book-sellers and manuscript collectors in London in the early twentieth century. It eventually ended up in the possession of British property developer, Howard Samuel, who was also a director of the socialist weekly *Tribune*, and who bought the pages for £2,300 in 1955. Today the pages are housed in the Karpeles Manuscript Library Museum in Santa Barbara, California. The pages had been part of the Kornik manuscript but had become detached from it before it was purchased by Dzialynski – the Duc de Bassano only verified twelve manuscript pages on 25 February 1822 (he probably did not count the thirteenth page which was only two lines long).

The fourth part of the manuscript (4), on pages 26–27 and 28–29 in this edition, was sent to Count Grigory Vladimirovich Orlov (1777–1826) by Hugues Maret, Duc de Bassano, in December 1823. It is preserved in the State Historical Museum in Moscow. Count Orlov, the nephew of Catherine the Great's favourites, Grigory and Alexei, was chamberlain and senator before spending time in France between 1810 and 1820. He was close to Emperor Napoleon's entourage (especially to Montholon) and he was a great collector of autographs, and gathered together Napoleon's handwritten manuscripts both before and after the latter's death. This fourth fragment was also published for the first time only by Fayard in 2007.

The fifth part of the manuscript (5) was only recently identified by Peter Hicks as the opening page of *Clisson and Eugénie*. A little over nineteen lines long, it appears on pages 13–14 of this English edition. Previously, the page, which had belonged to André de Coppet, a financier who amassed a significant collection of Napoleonic memorabilia in the early twentieth century (and also owned the third part of the manuscript before Howard Samuel), was believed to be part of a text that Napoleon had written about a historical figure named Clisson. The confusion arose partly because of Napoleon's sloppy handwriting. The page was auctioned in December 2007 for €24,000 to a private French collector. In the opinion of Peter Hicks and Émilie Barthet this page is the most polished version of the opening of the story, and it was also unpublished until the 2007 Fayard edition.

The sixth part (6) was also previously misidentified,

NOTE TO READERS

It has not been an easy task to reconstruct the text of *Clisson and Eugénie*. Napoleon himself put together only a draft, which nevertheless comprised the whole plot. Historians Albéric Cahuet and Simon Askenazy were able, with the manuscripts at their disposal, to establish only an outline of the story. Later the publishers of *Nouveau Fémina* and Girod de l'Ain slotted in the pages that had been lost and then rediscovered. Once that version of *Clisson and Eugénie* had been established, it was reproduced several times by various publishers until quite recently.

However, the discovery of new fragments put the established text in doubt. By merging the new manuscripts with the previously established version, we realised that not only did they describe new scenes but that they also contained reworkings of existing texts. This discovery meant that we had to compare all previous editions with the manuscripts. We proceeded by stages. Once the whole of the Askenazy manuscript had been verified, we had to choose from the various versions of the same passage. Where there were two or more versions of the same passage we chose the more polished one. We put the other less well-worked versions into the appendix of the French edition.

The most radical decision we faced concerned the beginning. The layout of the first page of Manuscript 2 seems to indicate Napoleon's indecision about how the story should begin. There are three versions of the beginning on that page without any intimation of which he preferred. In Manuscript 5, however, Napoleon appears to have found the way through his hesitations and the version here seems much more assured; we therefore published it as the opening to the novel.

On the other hand, there was not such a simple solution to the problems presented by Manuscript 4. In the end we decided to insert into Askenazy's outline some passages from Manuscript 4 and some passages from Manuscript 6. As a result, some of the new passages were put into the appendix of the French edition.

All the manuscripts were completely transcribed by us. We corrected numerous errors in the transcriptions made by Askenazy (helped by Arthur Chuquet, a historian and Napoleonic biographer) and by Girod de l'Ain. Although some gaps have been filled, there still remain some that will have to be tackled by future researchers.

Peter Hicks and Émilie Barthet

FURTHER READING

Christopher Frayling, *Napoleon Wrote Fiction* (Salisbury: Compton Press, 1972)

Steven Englund, *Napoleon: A Political Life* (Cambridge, Mass.: Harvard University Press, 2004)

John Holland Rose, *The Life of Napoleon I* (London: G. Bell & Sons, 1910; available to download at http://infomotions.com/etexts/gutenberg/dirs/1/4/3/0/14300/14300.htm)

John Holland Rose, *The Personality of Napoleon* (London: G. Bell & Sons, 1912; available to download at http://www.archive.org/details/personalityofnap00rose)

Vincent Cronin, *Napoleon* (London: Collins, 1971)

F. G. Healey, *The Literary Culture of Napoleon* (Geneva: Librairie E. Droz, 1959)

THE OFFICER'S PREY

The Napoleonic Murders

Armand Cabasson

June 1812. Napoleon begins his invasion of Russia leading the largest army Europe has ever seen.

But amongst the troops of the Grande Armée is a savage murderer whose bloodlust is not satisfied in battle.

When an innocent Polish woman is brutally stabbed, Captain Quentin Margont of the 84th Regiment is put in charge of a secret investigation to unmask the perpetrator. Armed with the sole fact that the killer is an officer, Margont knows that he faces a near-impossible task and the greatest challenge to his military career.

'Combines the suspense of a thriller with the compelling narrative of a war epic' *Le Parisien*

'Cabasson skilfully weaves an intriguing mystery into a rich historical background' *Mail on Sunday*

'. . . an enthralling and unromantic account of Napoleonic war seen from a soldier's perspective' *The Morning Star*

'. . . vivid portrayal of the Grande Armée . . .' *Literary Review*

'Cabasson's atmospheric novel makes a splendid war epic . . .' *Sunday Telegraph*

GALLIC BOOKS

978-1-906040-03-1

£7.99

WOLF HUNT

The Napoleonic Murders

Armand Cabasson

May 1809. The forces of Napoleon's Grande Armée are in Austria. For young Lieutenant Lukas Relmyer it is hard to return to the place where he and fellow orphan Franz were kidnapped four years earlier. Franz was brutally murdered and Lukas has vowed to avenge his death.

When the body of another orphan is found on the battlefield, Captain Quentin Margont and Lukas join forces to track down the wolf who is prowling once more in the forests of Aspern . . .

Winner of the Napoleon Foundation's fiction award 2005

GALLIC BOOKS

978-1-906040-08-6

£7.99

MEMORY OF FLAMES

The Napoleonic Murders

Armand Cabasson

March 1814. With the allied armies of Russia, Austria and Prussia advancing, Paris is in danger of falling to occupying forces for the first time in 400 years.

Following the murder of one of the colonels charged with defending the city, Joseph Bonaparte orders Lieutenant-Colonel Quentin Margont to conduct a secret investigation into the death.

A royalist emblem used by a group of monarchist conspirators has been found on the victim's horribly burned corpse; taking his life in his hands, Margont must now assume a false artistocratic identity in order to infiltrate the plotters.

And as his hunt for the killer progresses, the lieutenant-colonel uncovers a personal obsession for revenge which threatens to engulf the fate of Paris itself . . .

'With vivid scenes of battle and military life . . .'
Sunday Telegraph

GALLIC BOOKS

Paperback October 2009

978-1-906040-1-30

£7.99

Printed in the USA
CPSIA information can be obtained
at www.ICGtesting.com
JSHW031715140824
68134JS00038B/3699

9 781906 040277